Thank you to my Mommy who encouraged me to write this book, to my Daddy for always being by my side no matter what, and to my sister for inspiring a new bedtime story.
To the rest of my family, I love you!

Delaney the Dolphin's Dream
Copyright © 2024 by Brennan Hewlett
Illustrations by Brennan Hewlett

ISBN 9798333390523

Delaney the Dolphin's Dream

Written & Illustrated by Brennan Hewlett

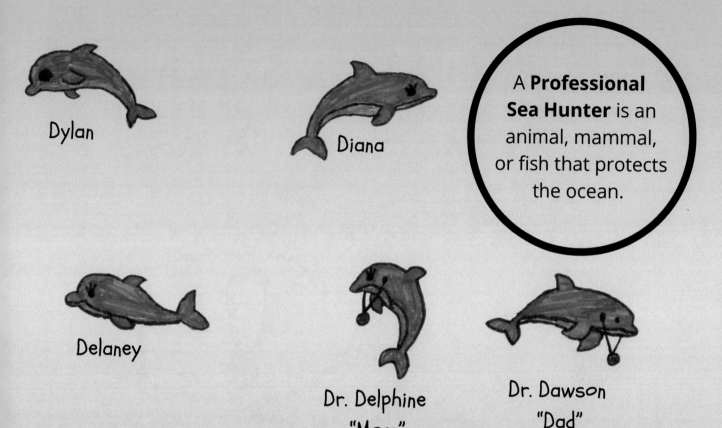

Dylan

Diana

A **Professional Sea Hunter** is an animal, mammal, or fish that protects the ocean.

Delaney

Dr. Delphine
"Mom"

Dr. Dawson
"Dad"

In Ocean City, there was a dolphin named Delaney. She had one older brother, Dylan, and one older sister, Diana, who cared deeply about her. Delaney's parents, Dr. Delphine and Dr. Dawson Dolphin, wanted her to be a doctor because they were the best doctors in the ocean.

But she had always dreamed of being a Professional Sea Hunter which was an important job in the NOP (National Ocean Protectors). Dylan and Diana encouraged her to be herself and to persevere through everything she tried. They always said, "anything is possible, as long as you try."

Every morning, Delaney and her best friend, Tiana the Turtle, swam together to school. That morning, Delaney was a little frustrated thinking about if her goal of becoming a Professional Sea Hunter would actually happen.

Tiana could tell Delaney was worried and told her, "anything is possible, as long as you try."
Delaney thought about the encouraging words the rest of the way to school.

At school, Delaney learned about ocean volcanoes and did a fun science experiment at school with her teacher, Mrs. Madison the Manatee. At the end of class, they were asked to write down what they wanted to be when they grew up.
Delaney knew exactly what to write.

Before she left the classroom, Mrs. Madison stopped Delaney and said she thought being a Professional Sea Hunter was wonderful. She told Delaney, "anything is possible, as long as you try."

When Delaney got home, she got ready for bed and drifted off to sleep quickly. She dreamed once again about being a Professional Sea Hunter.

The next day, Dylan and Diana took Delaney on an adventure.
They passed through...

Coral Reef

Seaweed Town

&

Sandy Lane

Until they got to a cave where everything was pitch black.

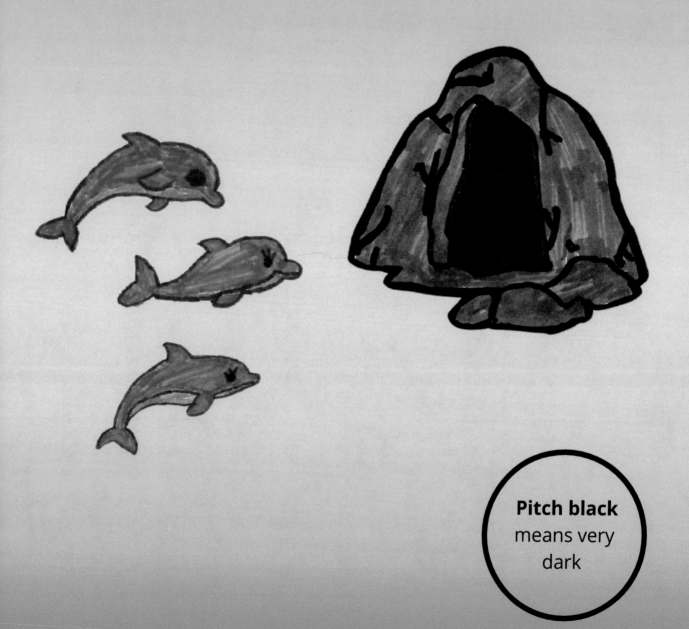

Pitch black means very dark

Delaney swam ahead of Dylan and Diana into the cave. Suddenly... BOOM! She turned around to see the rocks and mud crumbling at the entrance. As she swam deeper into the cave, Delaney saw two eyes looking at her. Delaney was worried and did not know what to do.
"Hello there! I'm Sam the Shark, a Professional Sea Hunter," came a voice from the shadows.

Crumbling means to break into pieces

Delaney bounced with joy.
She had never met anyone so awesome!

Delaney was excited to meet a new friend, but first, they had to get out of the cave.
The two pushed against the rocks for minutes until... CRASH!
They broke their way through!

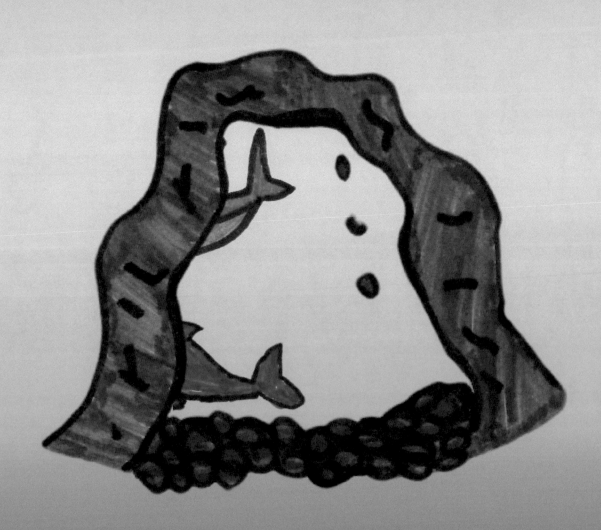

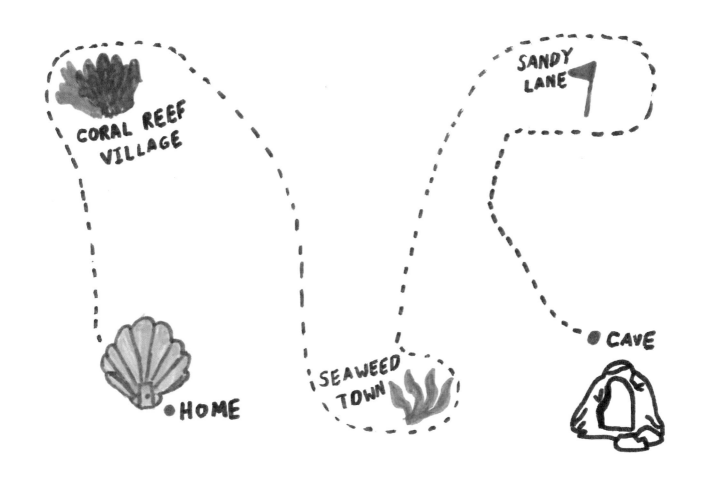

Delaney needed to find her way home. Delaney swam through Sandy Lane first, then Seaweed Town, and lastly Coral Reef Village. Finally, she made it home. It was a good thing she remembered those places from earlier that day.

When Delaney got home, she saw a marine biologist
swimming in front of her house.

The marine biologist needed a picture of a dolphin so Delaney
happily posed for the picture to help her. The marine biologist
waved thank you and swam up to the surface.

Delaney Dolphin

Delaney burst into her home, but the lights were off and no one seemed to be there.

"Congratulations!" her family yelled. Delaney was confused. Congratulations for what? Mom and Dad smiled and said, "We know how important becoming a Professional Sea Hunter is to you, so today, you've been taking tests to become a member of the NOP. You passed the Strength, Mapping, and Service exams!

Delaney was excited about her new job! She was ready to help protect the ocean and all of the animals.

At that moment, Delaney realized that dreams can really come true and that *anything is possible, as long she tries.*

Delaney's Dream was to be a Professional Sea Hunter.

What's your dream? Write or draw it below.

anything is
possible

AS LONG AS YOU TRY

Made in the USA
Middletown, DE
24 September 2024

61420408R00015